Teresa Ryckman lived in Ontario, Canada all her life. Throughout her childhood years, she was bullied by other children in her school. She is a survivor of spousal abuse and though her life endured a lot of painful moments, she always believed: "What gets you down, makes you stronger!" In believing that, she became more determined and focused on getting the most out of her life. She started writing, expressing all her feelings and emotions on paper to share with others and to let others know they are not alone and to never give up because your life is worth fighting for.

I dedicate this book to my family and those who experienced paranormal events.

Teresa Ryckman

THE DARK
EVIL ESSENCE

AUSTIN MACAULEY PUBLISHERS™

LONDON • CAMBRIDGE • NEW YORK • SHARJAH

Ordering Information
Quantity sales: Special discounts are available on quantity purchases by corporations, associations, and others. For details, contact the publisher at the address below.

Publisher's Cataloging-in-Publication data
Ryckman, Teresa
The Dark Evil Essence

ISBN 9798889105220 (Paperback)
ISBN 9798889105237 (Hardback)
ISBN 9798889105244 (ePub e-book)

Library of Congress Control Number: 2024900084

www.austinmacauley.com/us

First Published 2024
Austin Macauley Publishers LLC
40 Wall Street, 33rd Floor, Suite 3302
New York, NY 10005
USA

mail-usa@austinmacauley.com
+1 (646) 5125767

I would like to thank my family for their love and support. I like to thank Austin Macauley Publishers and all their staff for finding my work to be enthralling and unique. It's a great honor and I thank you for the publication of my book.

Prologue

As a child, Charles McGreevy lived an unhappy childhood. At the age of four years, his mother died of cancer. His father was unable to cope with the death of his wife, and would blame Charles for his mother's death. His father would torture him, leaving him with scars inside and out. Six years later, his father died of liver cancer. Charles was then placed in foster care throughout his childhood years and later was diagnosed with schizophrenia – a serious mental disorder in which people interpret reality abnormally.

Thirty years later, living in a physiological world filled with hate and anger deep within himself and toward those that were around him. He was a man that was never sociable with others and had always kept to himself. During the week, he would work in a factory distributing products to local distributors. Charles would put in a day's work, and then go home. At night, Charles would be home and would be in his den. He would pour himself a glass of brandy and sit in his black recliner chair with the remote to his television in one hand and his drink in the other. He would drink the evening away until he could no longer keep his eyes open.

His wife Clare, who had been married to Charles for six years, did not know much of his past life but only knew that he had a difficult upbringing and was raised through foster care. She would bring up his countless drinking habits, but that would only anger him and lead to violent attacks. One summer night, Clare ended up in ICU for three months with a fractured radius and two broken ribs, He threatened her that if she ever told anyone, the police, or even tried to leave him, he would kill her and their eight-year-old daughter Hannah. Clare felt trapped in the relationship and their daughter Hannah, filled with pure innocence, was trapped in a prison of misery.

On a cold winter's night, Clare and her daughter both were sleeping soundly in their beds, Charles suddenly woke up in a pool of sweat. The alcohol running through his veins and he was feeling disoriented. He staggered out of the den; he then walked toward the kitchen, while hearing his father's voice running through his head and telling him how worthless he is and that he was a walking mistake in this world. The glimpse of memories filled Charles's head with his father yelling and beating him continuously which made Charles feel emotionally distraught. Charles couldn't take it anymore so, he pulled a sharp knife from one of the kitchen drawers and walked upstairs into the bedrooms where his wife and child has slumbered. Then, feeling without remorse, he took the knife in his hand and plunged it forcefully into those that have loved him dearly.

Then, taking the knife upon himself and shouted, "You can't hurt me no longer!" and then, he slit his own throat. The blood was pouring out from his carotid artery and he started to feel the coldness throughout his body. He then, lay on the floor next to Clare and Hannah's bodies and slowly faded away into the darkness.

Chapter 1

It was the last bell of the day Alma Patterson would gather her books from her desk and start walking home. She lived a normal but unhappy childhood. Her unhappiness started when she attended St. Joseph Catholic School. The kids would tease her and make fun of her just cause she acted or looked different. She would sit at a table alone in the cafeteria while the other kids would sit in groups. During gym time, no one would be her partner when attending certain activities and during recess, she would sit on the concrete floor alone with her back up against the wall while everyone would play and be having fun.

For Christmas and Valentine's celebrations at school, all the kids would hand out Christmas or Valentine's Day cards. Alma would participate and hand out cards to each and every one in her class, all the cards would be placed in brown paper bags that were attached in front of every classmate's desk. Once all the cards were handed out, Alma would return to her desk and would find not one card in her brown paper bag. Alma sat down at her desk, with a sad look on her face, her heart heavy, and she felt emotionally devastated. For months, Alma would come home from school and cry in her mother's arms, not understanding why the kids were being so cruel.

It was getting close to the end of the year, with the summer holidays in just a few weeks. Alma's birthday was coming up on June 8th. Every month, her teacher, Mrs. Crawford, would announce the upcoming birthday in the classroom.

"We have two birthdays coming up for Zack and Alma!" announced Mrs. Crawford.

Alma could hear the girls whispering and laughing a couple of desks behind her. The girls in the classroom thought it would be a joke to play a trick on Alma by being nice and friendly and making her feel like she was part of their group. They would ask Alma to hang out with them during recess hour, would ask Alma to sit with them during lunch hour and the girls would ask Alma to be their partner during gym activities. For days, Alma was so happy and for the first time in a long time, she looked forward to going to school because the girl's made her feel like she belonged.

It was a week away before Alma's birthday, she felt so excited and was looking forward to handing out all her birthday invitations.

When she arrived at school, just before the bell rang, Alma walked into the classroom, took her birthday invitations out of her school bag, and placed one invitation on each of the girls' desks. When the bell rang, each of the girls walked to their desk, opened their invitations, and looked over toward Alma's direction, and with a smile, they each said, "Thank you!"

It was Saturday, June 8th, a day of celebrating Alma's birthday, and the party was set to begin at 12 o'clock. All the decorations were up, the food was displayed on the kitchen table, music playing in the background and all there was missing were the guest she invited.

It was 12:30 pm, and still no guests had shown up for Alma's party. Alma was starting to get worried. "Mom, no one has shown up yet!" said Alma.

"Don't worry hun, they will be here soon!" replied her Mom.

Sure enough, it was 1 O'clock and none of the guests came. Alma was so upset, she ran upstairs into her room, slammed her bedroom door shut, lay on her bed, and started crying.

All the girls that Alma had invited to her party, had led her to believe that they were her friends and made her feel like she was part of something special.

Alma's parents walked up the stairs and opened her bedroom door and her mother sat by her bedside while her father stood still and leaned up against the door frame of Alma's bedroom door.

Alma explained to her parents what the girls in her classroom did and how they made her feel leading up to her special day. Her Mom and Dad were upset and heartbroken about what had happened to their daughter. Alma's Mom held her in her arms and told her everything was going to be OK.

For months after, Alma felt more depressed. She hated going to school and never wanted to go outside by any means. When she did go outside, it would only be for family functions that she would have to attend.

Her parents, Vince and Anne, would be concerned about their angel and it broke their hearts to see their child in such disparity. They wanted the best for their both children and happiness was one of them.

Alma's father worked as a postal clerk for the Whitby Post Office for twenty years. When Alma was sick and stayed home from school, her father would bring home some kids magazines and a box of french fries from 'Harriet's Fish and Chips'. She would think it was the best part of being sick and staying home. She would always be "Daddy's Little Girl."

Alma's mother worked as a Medical Receptionist for the Whitby Clinic for twelve years. Like her father, she would always be there for her and her brother at a time when needed; Alma believed her mother would have a special technique of healing. When she or her brother would feel sad, her mother always knew what to do and what to say to make things right again. Alma would always be 'Her Little Angel.'

Vince and Anne decided it was time to sell the house and move to a new location. It was not only in the best interests and accommodation wise for the Patterson family but also for Alma to start a new beginning and to have an opportunity to start a new school and make new friends.

After months of the 'For sale' sign being up, the house finally sold.

Vince and Anne purchased a small bungalow home in Whitby on Hutchinson Ave. The Patterson family was excited about their new home, and Vince and Anne knew a fresh start is what they needed not only for themselves but also for their children. They both felt things would turn for the better or...did they?

Chapter 2

Driving up the driveway to their new home, Vince and Anne decided to walk inside while the movers unload the furniture. In the entryway, there were two sections of the house. One section was stairs leading to the basement and the other section was stairs leading to the main level. Vince and Anne went down the stairs to the basement and at the bottom of the stairs, across the room, was the furnace room. Over to the right, down the hall was the kitchen and family room. Left of the family room, there were these bi-fold western-type doors that lead to the parlor gameroom. In the center of this room was a pool table with a felt green tarp, the pool cues were hanging off the cue rack and there was a chalkboard on the wall to keep score. On the right of the room was the bathroom and laundry room.

Vince and Anne walked up the stairs to take a look at the main level of their new home.

At the top of the stairs was the living room for when the Patterson's invite family and friends over. Down the hall to the right, was the second kitchen with a bigger open area to place a large dining table.

"Having a second kitchen in this house could come in handy!" Anne mentioned to Vince.

"Especially when we have big family functions such as Christmas, Thanksgiving, and other special events!" replied Vince.

As both Anne and Vince continued walking the main level, down the hallway to the left, was a doorway leading to the master bedroom. The room had his and her walk-in closet and a beautiful ensuite with a large Roman tub. Further down from Vince and Anne's bedroom was a doorway leading to another bedroom for their son Joe. Joe was three years older than Alma and as a brother, he would help her at times with her schoolwork and he would even be there for Alma as any big brother would.

At the end of the hall, there was another bathroom, and beside the bathroom was Alma's bedroom. Alma was in her room, putting her clothes away and displaying her dolls on the dresser. Alma looked up and saw her parents standing in front of her doorway and with a smile, she continued to put all her things away in her room.

Vince and Anne left the kids' rooms and decided to finish unpacking all their boxes and start organizing each room.

After Alma displayed all her dolls on the dresser, Alma decided to put her shoes on and go outside in the backyard. Outside, there was a gate opening between the garage and the house which lead to the backyard. Alma unlatched the gate and started walking toward the backyard when Alma noticed a brown shed on the right against the back fence and a swing set in the middle. Alma also saw her new school on the other side of their backyard fence. Alma walked over toward the swing set and sat down on one of the swings. Alma swayed back and forth on the swing set. As she went higher and higher, she would think that she could touch the clouds with her feet if she went high enough. Feeling the breeze on her face and through her long brown hair as Alma was swinging back and forth, she caught a glimpse at one of the back windows of her house. She saw a shadowy like figure peering through the white curtain sheers that were hanging in her bedroom window. Thinking in her mind that it was her Mom checking on her while she was in the backyard. Alma jumped off her swing and started walking back toward the front of the house and went inside.

Vince and Anne were still putting things away and Joe decided to grab the rest of his belongings from the front foyer. As Joe was grabbing his boxes, he started hearing scratching sounds coming from the basement. As Joe walked down the stairs, the scratching sound became louder and was coming from the furnace room.

Chapter 3

As Joe got closer, the scratching sound stopped. The room was dark as night, Joe's heart began to race, and he felt a chill going up his spine so, he decided to turn back and leave the furnace room. Suddenly, a hand touched his shoulder and Joe was completely frightened and startled by the touch, he turned around and it was his father standing before him.

"What are you doing down here?" asked his father.

"I heard scratching sounds coming from the furnace room!" replied Joe.

Vince turned his flashlight on and pointed it toward the switch on the wall. He then turned the light on and looked around the furnace room, but nothing was there.

"You must have been hearing things!" said his Dad.

They both started to exit the furnace room when they both started hearing scratching sounds. The sound was coming from behind the storage boxes. They both walked toward the storage boxes; Vince flashed his flashlight in the direction where the scratching sounds were coming from and out jumped a black cat. Feeling startled but relieved, they both looked at each other and started to laugh. Feeling silly to have thought that there was something scary inside the furnace room. Joe picked up the black stray cat and held it in his arms; the cat began purring with contentment.

"Can we keep him?" asked Joe.

"We have to get him checked by the doctor, if he has a clean bill of health from the veterinarian, you and Alma can keep him," replied Vince.

Vince then walked upstairs to help Anne finish unpacking while Joe took the new family member upstairs and into Alma's room to show her their new family pet.

Meanwhile, Vince was telling Anne what had happened in the basement, both laughing as they put the dishes away in the kitchen cupboard.

"I'm glad we did this, hon, selling the house and moving here," said Anne.

Vince took Anne's hand, pulled her close, and said, "Everything is going to be OK!" as he embraced her in his arms.

"I hope so babe, I hope so," replied Anne.

In Alma's room, she and Joe were playing with the cat.

"What should we call him?" she asked Joe.

"What about Shadow?"

"Dad and I found him in the shadows, by the boxes in the furnace room," replied Joe.

"Yeah…let's call him Shadow!" said Alma as she hugged the cat close.

It was getting late and the Patterson family just finished dinner. Alma walked into her room and put her pajamas on and then went into the bathroom to brush her teeth. Anne washed up the dishes while Vince dried them from the dishrack. Joe, lay on his bed with his headphones on, listening to music while Shadow lay at the foot of his bed.

After drying the dishes, both Anne and Vince sat down on the couch and watched a bit of television before going to bed. Alma walked downstairs in her pajamas, toward her parents to give them a goodnight kiss. Alma walked back upstairs into her bedroom, placed her favorite doll on her night table, said her prayers, laid down on her bed and fell asleep.

Chapter 4

It was a beautiful September morning, the summer holidays had ended and it was back to school for Joe and Alma. It was 7:30 am, the alarm went off in Anne's bedroom and it was time to get up to get the kids ready for their first day of school. Joe was already dressed and was sitting at the kitchen table eating his breakfast. Alma, who seemed to be dragging her feet in the morning finally got out of bed, got dressed in the clothes that her mother bought for her to wear on her first day and then walked into the kitchen and sat down to eat her breakfast.

Her mother noticed how quiet Alma was during breakfast, she had the feeling that something was bothering her.

"Is everything OK, Alma?" her mother asked.

"Just nervous about school," replied Alma.

"Everything is going to be fine. You're going fine!" said Anne.

"But what if they don't like me?" asked Alma.

"They will, my angel! Don't you worry! Just be yourself," her mom replied. Anne gave her daughter a big hug and a kiss on her forehead. She then looked at Alma with a smile and said, "You're my angel and I love you!"

"I love you too, Mommy!" replied Alma.

With a smile, Alma stood up from the kitchen table, went to the bathroom to brush her teeth, and walked toward the foyer. She then put on her shoes and jacket, grabbed her backpack off the bench rack, gave her mom a hug and kiss, and started walking to school.

As Alma walked up the sidewalk toward the school, she thought about what her mother had said and started feeling less nervous about going to school.

It was 8:30 am, the school bell rang and school was about to start. Alma hung her jacket on the hook in the school hallway and walked inside the classroom.

Her teacher, Miss. Polanski welcomed Alma in front of the class. This was Miss. Polanski's second year of teaching grade 2 at St. Theresa's Catholic School.

"Class, this is Alma Patterson!"

"She's new here to this school and I want you all to welcome her!" said Miss Polanski.

"Hi, Alma!" announced the class.

"Alma, you may take your seat," said Miss. Polanski.

Alma walked toward the desk that she was assigned to and sat down.

The girl next to her leaned over and with a smile said, "Hi! My name is Melissa Park."

"Hi!" replied Alma.

"Do you want to play with me and my friends during recess?" asked Melissa.

Alma smiled and said, "Yes! I would like that."

"Great!" replied Melissa.

Melissa smiled back at Alma and then turned to face the front of the class.

Meanwhile, back at the house, Anne thought that since the kids were in school and Vince was at work, she was going to clean and organize the household before everyone came home at the end of the day.

She decided to take a shower first; so, she grabbed a towel from the linen closet and placed it on the vanity in the bathroom. She grabbed a change of clothes from her walk-in closet and placed them on her bed. Anne locked the front and side door of the house and feeling secure, she then walked down the hall, toward her bedroom, and into her ensuite. She turned the faucets on in the shower, took her robe off, and closed the shower door behind her. While in the shower, Anne could feel a sense that someone was watching her.

She would look through the glass shower door but, no one was there. Thinking nothing much of it, Anne continued taking her shower. Once Anne was done bathing in the shower, she turned the faucets off, grabbed her towel from the vanity, and started drying herself off. As she was drying herself off, she heard footsteps coming from the other side of her bathroom door. Anne opened the bathroom door, she looked around her bedroom but no one was there. She walked over toward her bed, got dressed, hung her towel on the towel rack, and walked out her bedroom door. As she walked down the hallway, she started hearing a knocking sound coming from the front door. Anne walked over toward the front door, she began to open the door but no one was there. She closed the front door and as she walked away, there was another but, louder. She opened the front door, and again, no one was there. Anne walked down the porch steps and around the corner she looked around and saw nothing. Anne walked back into the house and locked the door behind her.

Anne looked at the clock on the stove and noticed that it was almost 12 o'clock. She started cleaning up the house before everyone came home around 3:30 pm.

It was 2:30 pm, everything was organized and all that needed to be done were the beds. She finished doing up her and Joe's bed and all that was left was Alma's bed. Once Alma's bed was done, it was time to start dinner. Anne walked out of Alma's bedroom, she walked down the hallway, and into the kitchen to start making dinner.

It was 3:30 pm, Vince and the children came home and dinner was ready to be placed on the table.

After showering, Vince got dressed, walked into the kitchen and wrapped his arms around Anne, and gave her a kiss on the cheek.

"How was your day, sweetheart? I see you have been busy!" said Vince as he walked over and sat down at the dinner table.

"I was able to get most of the work done today," replied Anne.

"You must have been really busy! That would explain why the beds didn't get done up!" Vince said sarcastically. Anne turned to Vince with a confused look on her face.

"The beds were done up! I did all the beds up before I started dinner!" Anne said in an annoyed response.

Vince told her to go take a look in the bedrooms. Anne walked out of the kitchen and into their bedroom and noticed that the blanket and sheets on the bed were messed up. Feeling confused, Anne also walked into Joe and

Alma's bedroom and noticed the same thing, the blankets and sheets on their beds were a mess.

"I'm pretty sure I have done up all the beds today, I know I did!" Anne told Vince in an upsetting voice.

"Don't worry babe! You had a lot on your plate today! I'm home tomorrow, I will help you finish up with everything!" said Vince as he held Anne in his arms.

It was dinner time, the Patterson family sitting together at the dinner table and each was discussing to one about their day.

"How was your first day at school guys?" asked Vince.

"Good!" Joe replied as he reached over to grab a dinner roll.

"Alma. What about you?" asked her dad.

"Great!" replied Alma as she poured a glass of milk for herself.

"Really?" asked her Mom.

"Yeah! There is this girl in my class, named Melissa. She and I played together with her friends during recess. I had a lot of fun!" Alma said cheerfully.

Vince and Anne were so happy for their little angel.

After dinner, Joe and Alma went into their bedrooms to do homework while Vince helped Anne with the dishes.

While doing the dishes, Anne was explaining the unusual situation that happened today while everyone was gone. She told Vince about while in the shower, she felt like someone was watching her and that she heard footsteps outside her bathroom door. She also told him that someone was knocking at the front door and when she opened the front door, no one was there.

"That's odd!" said Vince.

"I too found that to be weird as well!" responded Anne.

Vince told Anne that the house is old and when the house shifts, it tends to make creaking sounds from the floor or through the walls. He told her it was probably nothing and not to worry about it.

Vince and Anne were done doing the dishes together and decided to go into the living room and sit down on the couch, cuddle up, and watch some television before going to bed.

Joe was done doing his homework in his room and decided to call his girlfriend, Kim. While talking on the phone, Joe heard a faint knocking sound coming from the other side of his bedroom door, "Kim, hang on a sec!" said Joe.

Joe placed the phone down on his bed and walked toward his bedroom door. He opened the door but no one was there; so, thinking nothing of it, he closed his bedroom door and picked up the phone from his bed and continued talking to his girlfriend.

A few minutes later, a louder knock came from Joe's bedroom door.

"One sec, Kim!" Joe annoyingly said.

Joe placed the phone down again on the bed and walked over toward his bedroom door. Joe opened the door and no one was there. Joe started getting frustrated; he closed the door and walked away. As he started walking back toward the phone on his bed, an even louder knock was coming from Joe's door. He aggressively opened the door and still no one was there. Thinking that his little sister was playing tricks on him, he went to check on Alma in her bedroom but Alma was not even in her room. Alma was sitting with her mom and dad on the couch watching television. Joe, feeling confused, returned to his bedroom and shut the door behind him.

It was getting late, it was time for everyone to go to bed. Alma brushed her teeth and both her parents tucked her into bed. Vince and Anne walked over to Joe's bedroom to say 'Goodnight' to him and then they both walked into their bedroom and said 'Goodnight' to each other as they then fell asleep.

Chapter 5

The next morning, Vince woke up early to make breakfast for the kids and have them ready for school. Once Joe and Alma left for school, Vince tidied up the kitchen and started making breakfast for Anne and himself. Anne woke up to a delicious aroma scent that filled the air. The scent was coming from the kitchen; so, she grabbed her robe off the slipper chair and walked out from the bedroom and into the kitchen.

"Good morning!" said Anne.

"Good morning, my love. How did you sleep?" replied Vince.

"I slept really good, thank you!" Anne said, with a smile.

They both sat down together at the kitchen table, eating their breakfast while enjoying each other's company.

After breakfast, Anne cleared the dishes from the kitchen table and started washing them while Vince gathered the cardboard boxes that were used to move into the house and also the garbage from the kitchen bin, and took it out to the garage.

While Anne was finishing up in the kitchen, she heard a loud 'shatter' coming from the living room. She turned the faucets off, dried the counter top and went to go take a look to see what had happened. There, she saw her wedding photo of her and Vince, broken pieces of glass that were scattered on the floor. The picture frame was given as a wedding gift on the day of their wedding from her Grandmother. It was very sentimental to both her and Vince…feeling upset and disappointed with what had happened, she carefully picked up the shards of glass and removed the wedding photo before throwing the picture frame out. She then placed the photo in her bedroom, on the tall dresser, until she can buy another frame for it. She did up her bed while she was in the room and then went into Joe and Alma's bedroom to clean up and do their beds. Anne walked out of the kid's bedroom and into the living room, where she saw her husband Vince through the bay window, talking to one of the neighbors on the street. Anne put on her jacket and shoes and walked out the front door to meet her new neighbors.

Outside, Vince introduced his wife, Anne to Don and Jane Madeline. Don and Jane were a happily married couple with two children, who lived on Hutchinson Avenue for twenty years. During the conversation, Vince and Anne got the impression that the couple seemed very intuitive about them and their house. At the end of their conversation, Vince and Anne said 'Good Bye' to Don and Jane and walked back toward their house. While walking their way back, Anne told Vince about the wedding photo falling off the end table in the living room and the glass frame that shattered on the floor. As disappointing as it was, they decided to go out the next day to buy a new frame.

Vince went downstairs to watch the hockey game on television while Anne decided to get dinner ready before the kids came home. In the kitchen, cooking supper, Anne heard another glass-shattering sound coming from one of the bedrooms. Anne turned the stove element to a low setting and walked down the hallway to check the bedrooms. She checked her bedroom, there was nothing on the bedroom floor or on the ensuite floor. She then checked Joe and Alma's bedroom and noticed a porcelain figurine had fallen off Alma's triple dresser and shattered into pieces on the bedroom floor. Anne looked around, feeling unsure what had caused the figurine to break when out came Shadow, the black cat running out from underneath Alma's bed.

The cat startled Anne, causing her heart and pulse to race.

"Stupid cat!" said Anne in an annoyed voice.

As Anne bent down to pick up the porcelain pieces off the floor, she felt a cold chill, shivering up her spine. The temperature in the room felt colder than the rest of the rooms in the household. Thinking nothing of it, Anne stood up with the pieces in her hand and started walking out toward the bedroom door. She did not know that behind her, there was a dark evil essence peering through Alma's triple dresser mirror, and was watching Anne as she walked out into the hallway.

It was 3:30 pm, Joe and Alma came home from school, and Vince walked upstairs and into the kitchen to see when dinner will be ready.

Anne had dinner ready and was serving it on the dinner table while Vince and the kids washed up in the bathroom before sitting down at the table.

At the kitchen table, Anne told Alma about her porcelain figurine and about Shadow knocking it over. She then told the kids to keep their bedroom door closed at all times, so that Shadow won't be able to knock down any of their items over and break them.

After dinner, Vince helped Anne with the dishes while Joe and Alma went into their bedrooms to do their homework.

After the dishes, Vince and Anne walked into the living room and sat on the couch to watch some television before going to bed. Joe finished his homework, got changed into his pajamas, brushed his teeth in the bathroom, and then walked down the hallway, toward the living room to watch some television with his parents before going to bed. It was getting late, Vince turned the television off, Anne and Joe walked toward their bedroom doors and said 'Good night' to one another.

Vince walked up the stairs, toward his bedroom, and stopped in the middle of the hallway. He heard Alma's voice, talking and laughing in her bedroom. Vince walked quietly and closer to Alma's bedroom door. Listening closely, he heard Alma having a conversation with someone on the other side. He grabbed the door handle to open the door,

"Alma, who are you talking to?" asked her father.

"I'm talking to Hannah, Daddy!" said Alma.

Vince looked around the room and saw no one but Alma in the room. "Who's Hannah?" asked her father in a curious voice.

"She's my friend! She lives here in our house too," replied Alma.

"I…see," Vince responded in a confused voice.

"Well, it's time for bed; so go brush your teeth in the bathroom, put your pajamas on, and get ready for bed." Vince told her.

Alma stood up from her bedroom floor, walked into the bathroom, and brushed her teeth; she then put her pajamas on and got into bed.

Vince, tucked Alma into bed, gave her a kiss on the forehead, and said 'Good night' to Alma. He took another glance around the room before walking out of Alma's bedroom door.

Vince brushed his teeth in the ensuite, he glanced over toward his bed and saw Anne sitting up in the bed, with her back leaned up against the headboard while reading her book.

Chapter 6

Vince took his robe off, crawled into bed and reached over toward Anne, and gave her a kiss good night on the cheek. Vince lay in bed, thinking about Alma and who she was talking to in her bedroom. Anne finished a chapter in her book and placed it on the end table by her bedside; she looked over and notice her husband gazing up at the ceiling.

"Is everything alright, hon?" asked Anne.

Vince told Anne about Alma talking to someone in her bedroom and how odd it was to hear her having a conversation with someone that was not even there. Anne told Vince to not worry and that she will talk to Alma in the morning. Anne leaned over, gave Vince a kiss on the lips, and told him to get some rest. Anne leaned over on her side and turned the bedside lamp off.

Chapter 7

For several months, the Patterson family had experienced paranormal events in their home. These events became more aggressive and sometimes even violent toward the family, making them feel frightened and deeply distraught.

It was late in the evening, Anne grabbed the laundry from the laundry room, then went upstairs to the main level of the house and placed the laundry basket by the doorway that lead to her bedroom. She continued walking down the hallway to check on Joe and Alma before getting ready for bed. After checking on the children, Anne grabbed her laundry basket and walked into her bedroom. She noticed Vince was already sleeping, she walked into the ensuite to brush her teeth and get ready for bed.

Anne tried to settle in for the night but she felt so overwhelmed and perplexed in her thoughts, her emotions and feelings became restless and unsettled. Within moments, as Anne lay in bed, she settled into a deep sleep, and within her self-conscious mind, she developed a disturbing dream.

A dark evil essence was approaching her as she felt a cold chilling sensation throughout her whole body. She felt paralyzed, unable to make any sudden movement with her legs or arms. Anne wanted to yell out 'Help' but she remained speechless, unable to utter words or make a sound. There was a total feeling of helplessness and fear within her. As the dark evil essence approached Anne closer to grab her, she finally managed to let out a sharp, piercing scream. Anne woke up feeling terrified, her body in a cold sweat and her heart pulsating. Her husband, awaken from Anne's nightmare, leaned over and turned the table lamp on.

"Are you alright?" Vince asked.

"I had a horrible nightmare!" replied Anne in a trembling voice,

Vince held his wife close into his arms and comfort her as she explained her nightmare. Once Vince was able to calm Anne's emotional distress, they both lay down in bed and tried to get some rest.

The next morning, Vince dropped Joe and Alma off at school while on his way to work. Anne finished her breakfast, she washed all the dishes, dried them, and put them away in the kitchen cabinet. She then went into her bedroom to get dressed and ready for work. Anne started to hear movements in the kitchen, as though someone was walking and shuffling things around. Anne walked out of her bedroom and into the kitchen, and noticed all her dishes were removed from the cabinet and were displayed on the countertop and all the cutlery that was in the drawers were displayed in a pentagram shape on the floor. Anne, feeling frightened, grabbed her jacket, shoes, and purse and walked out of the house.

On the way to work, she called Vince on the car phone and told him what had happened while she was getting ready for work. He told her to stop by the post office after she was done work and they would drive home together.

After work, as Vince and Anne drove up the driveway, they noticed their garage door was opened. Vince and Anne got out of the car and walked toward the garage. There they saw Anne's brother, Steve, grabbing tools from the tool chest. Anne's brother was the CEO of his own Aluminum Siding Company and needed some materials for a job site.

"Hey, Steve! How are you?" asked Vince.

"I'm good, thanks!" replied Steve.

During their conversation with Steve, Vince and Anne explained to him what was happening inside their house and asked him for his opinion on how to handle the situation.

Steve told them that paranormal activity was not uncommon and that they need to do a complete background check on the house to find out what had happened and what kind of entity it was that they were dealing with. At the end of their conversation, they said bye to Steve and went inside the house. Vince and Anne walked upstairs, into the kitchen and noticed all the dishes and cutlery that Anne described how they were displayed were now all put away and were back in the cabinet.

Both Vince and Anne walked into their bedroom, Vince went to take a shower while Anne got changed into her comfortable clothes and walked out of the bedroom and into the kitchen to start dinner before the children came home.

Joe and Alma arrived home from school, they both went into their rooms to change out of their school clothes and into their pajamas; both washed up for supper and sat down at the kitchen table with their mom and dad.

After dinner, Alma went into her room to play with her dolls; Joe finished his homework and was then talking on the phone with his girlfriend. Anne cleared the table and washed the dishes while Vince sat down and watched the hockey game on the television. Once the dishes were done, Anne went downstairs and into the basement to grab something from the freezer. As she was walking down the stairs, a strong pungent decaying smell filled the air, making it unbearable to breathe. She turned the light on at the bottom of the stairs, Anne walked around to find out where the stench was coming from but she was unable to locate where it was, so she grabbed what she needed from the freezer and walked back up the stairs.

It was getting late, Vince turned the television off and walked out of the living room and toward his bedroom to get ready for bed. Anne decided to check on Joe and Alma before going to bed herself. She checked on Joe and Alma and they both were nestled in their beds and asleep. Anne walked into her bedroom to put her nightgown on and crawled into bed.

The hours passed within the night, around 3:30 am, Anne woke up with a sudden urge to check on her children. She checked on Alma first, she was sleeping soundly in her bed. Anne then went to check on her son Joe, but he was not in his bed or in his bedroom. She suddenly heard noises coming from the kitchen, so Anne walked toward the kitchen and saw her son standing on a chair, close to the stove with all four burners turned on. In a subconscious state, Joe was unaware of the surrounding danger he was about to face. Anne knew not to startle her son, so she walked over to him slowly and turned all four burners off.

She then placed both her hands on her son's shoulders and guided him slowly back into bed.

Once Joe was back in his bed, Anne sat down on his bedside, feeling a sense of relief that her son was not injured, she leaned over and kissed him on his forehead, and walked out from his bedroom and into her bedroom.

For several hours, Anne would lay in bed, unable to calm her mind, and the feeling of anxiety and agitation was causing her to be restless and unable to fall asleep.

It was 6 am and her husband's alarm clock turned on.

Vince turned his alarm clock off and noticed his wife was sitting up in bed, with her back up against the headboard and her table lamp light on.

"What's the matter? Why are you awake?" asked Vince.

Anne explained what happened in the middle of the night and the inner sense she felt to check on the children. She told her husband that their son was standing over the stove, with all four burners turned on and without knowing in his subconscious mind, that he was in danger. Vince was having mixed emotions of feeling angry and scared, but there was a sense of relief he felt that his son was not seriously injured.

Vince and Anne decided that in the morning, after breakfast, they will drop both their children off at their grandparents for a while and take a drive up to the Whitby Public Library.

They considered to take Anne's brother's advice and do complete research on the house.

Chapter 8

Before driving to the Whitby Public Library, Vince and Anne dropped their children off first at their grandparents and got them settled, then decided to drive toward Jakob's Cafe and picked up a coffee for them both. After they had their coffee, they drove to the Public library and parked their car in one of the parking lots in front of the building all walked inside. Inside the library, Vince and Anne walked toward the section where the microfilm machines were; they both sat down on one of the chairs and started doing the background research on their home.

For a while, Vince and Anne searched through the microfilm and finally came across a newspaper clipping about a brutal murder in Whitby, that took place in a house about ten years ago and claimed the lives of three victims. As they continue reading the newspaper clipping, it indicated that a family by the name of McGreevy, lived in the house on 901 Hutchinson Avenue and the Whitby Police Department the Paramedics, and the Forensic Team were all called to the scene one cold evening night and found three bodies brutally murdered.

One of the witnesses that was being questioned at the scene stated, the husband and wife were not very sociable and had always kept to themselves and their daughter rarely went outside of their home. The mother was brutally murdered in the master bedroom and her body was stabbed multiple times. The daughter was found in her bedroom, her body was also stabbed multiple times. Both bodies were found together in the master bedroom. The Captain, head of the police department, stated that this was a 'vicious attack!' He claimed, the bodies were beyond recognition when found. The culprit, behind the two murders, was the husband and his body was found in the master bedroom beside the bodies of his wife and child. He took his own life after taking the life of his wife and daughters.

As Vince and Anne read the column, the story also told that Mr. Charles McGreevy had lived an unhappy childhood. At the age of four, his mother died of cancer. His father, who was unable to cope with the death of his wife, would blame Charles for his mother's death. His father would torture him, leaving him with scars inside and out. Six years later, his father died of liver cancer. Charles was then placed in Foster Care throughout his childhood years. He was diagnosed with schizophrenia, a serious mental disorder.

Thirty years later, living a physiological world filled with hate, and anger and feeling the inner darkness, he developed a sense of evil deep within himself.

During the day, Charles lived what seemed to be a normal life. He would work in a factory, distributing products to local distributors. At night, he was at home, in his den, sitting in his black chair, and would always pour himself a glass of brandy. He would drink the evening away till he could no longer keep his eyes open.

His wife, Clare, who had been married to Charles for six years, did not know about his past life, but only knew that he had a difficult upbringing and was raised through Foster Care. Clare would bring up his countless drinking habits, but doing so led to violent attacks from her husband. One summer night, she ended up in ICU for three months. Charles threatened his wife and said that if she ever told anyone, including authorities or even left him, he would kill her and their eight-year-old daughter Hannah. Clare felt trapped like an animal in a cage and her daughter, full of pure innocence, was also trapped in misery.

Late one night, while Clare and her daughter Hannah, were sleeping peacefully in their beds, Charles suddenly woke up in a cold sweat, he had the unpleasant smell of alcohol on his body, and with having medical condition of schizophrenia, he would hear voices in his head from his abused father, taunting him continuously that one evening night, he couldn't take it anymore and walked toward the kitchen, grabbed one of the knives from the drawers, walked into the bedrooms of where his love ones would slumber and he plunged the knife repeatedly into his wife and daughter before taking his own life. The autopsy showed that Charles' injury was caused by a self-inflicted wound across his neck, severing the carotid artery and leading him to bleed out.

After reading the article, Vince and Anne looked at each other, both were having an unpleasant feeling in their stomachs, they both knew something had to be done for the certainty of their safety and well-being for them and for their two children.

On the way home from the library, Vince and Anne continued their discussion about the history and events that took place in their home and decided to keep the information to themselves and from their children for the time being. They felt, the information they gathered would only be upsetting to the children and create a lot of unanswered questions from family members and Vince and Anne are not prepared to deal with that.

Chapter 9

After picking the children up on the way home from their grandparents, Vince helped Anne prepare dinner and set the dinner table. Joe was in his room, on his computer while Alma was sitting in the living room watching television. After dinner, Vince helped Anne clear the dishes from the table and as she washed the dishes, her husband would dry them. Both talked about the article when the children were not around. Deep down, with the paranormal events happening, they knew things would only get worst and the only solution was to have their home blessed by a priest. Vince cut the conversation short with Anne suddenly because he saw their son Joe walking toward the kitchen.

"What were you guys talking about?" asked Joe.

"Oh, nothing important!" replied his father.

"Let's go watch some television while your mother finishes up!" suggested his father.

Vince and Joe walked out of the kitchen and into the living room, sat down on the couch, and watched a movie while Anne finished drying the dishes and putting them away.

Alma was playing in her bedroom with her dolls when she noticed her ghostly friend Hannah peering out from her bedroom closet.

"Come play with me, Hannah!" said Alma with a smile.

Alma knew her friend Hannah was different from all her other friends at school. She never told any of her friends about Hannah because she felt they wouldn't understand and would only make fun of her.

While playing dolls with Hannah, Alma could hear her mother calling her name from outside her bedroom door. As Alma was getting up and walking toward her bedroom door to open it, Hannah saw a dark ghostly apparition peering through Alma's dresser mirror. It was Hannah's father that had been taunting her human friend and her family. Hannah knew that as long as her friend Alma and her family stay in the house, they would be in danger. Without being able to warn her friend, Hannah shifted toward where Alma was standing and protect her from her father. Alma, without acknowledgment of what was behind her, she walked out toward her mother.

Alma walked into the kitchen where her mother was standing and was making herself a cup of tea.

"Yes, Mommy?" said Alma.

"It's time for you to brush your teeth and get ready for bed!" replied her mother.

Alma walked back down the hallway and into the bathroom to brush her teeth, and then went into her bedroom. When entering the bedroom, Alma noticed her friend was nowhere in her room. Alma grabbed her pajamas from her dresser, got dressed, and crawled into her bed.

It was getting late, Joe walked down the hallway and into the bathroom to brush his teeth while Vince turned the television off and checked to make sure all the doors were locked before getting ready for bed.

Anne finished drinking the tea she made and placed her cup in the sink. She checked to make sure all the lights were turned off in the living room when she noticed one of the lamps was flickering. Thinking it was just a loose light bulb, she decided to tighten the bulb to fix the light. She felt the temperature suddenly change in the room, the same foul decay smell that was once in the basement was now in the presence of where she stood and as she turned her body around…there, hovering before her was the dark evil essence. Anne screamed and ran toward her bedroom and into her husband's arms.

"What happened?" Vince asked in a concerned voice.

"The dark image that was in my nightmare, was standing in the living room!" Anne replied in a shaken voice.

Vince grabbed his housecoat and with Anne by his side, they both walked out from the bedroom and toward the living room.

Vince turned on all the lights in each room and saw nothing. He comfort his wife and both walked back toward their bedroom. Anne got dressed and crawled next to her husband in bed. She felt safe in her husband's arms knowing that with him by her side, no one could hurt her. She left one of her table lamps on as a night light and tried to fall asleep.

Moments later, as Anne lay in her bed, she heard a loud scream coming from her daughter's bedroom. She awakened her husband and told him that she heard a loud scream coming from their daughter's bedroom. Both got out of bed to check on their daughter when suddenly they could hear their daughter screaming, calling for help from the other side of the bedroom door. Vince tried to open the door but it would not open.

"Hang on, sweety! Daddy's coming!" yelled out her father.

"Daddy, hurry! He is hurting me!" cried Alma.

Vince tried to run at the bedroom door with all his body weight and finally the bedroom door swung open. Vince and Anne were shocked and frightened by what they saw when the door opened. There, their daughter hanging on the footboard post for dear life while the dark evil essence had a grip on Alma's ankle as he tried to pull her closer. Alma screams 'Help!' Vince tried to grab his daughter and pull her toward him and away from the yips of the evil apparition. Vince did not have enough strength to pull his daughter close, so Anne helped her husband and both were able to pull their daughter away from the evil spirit. The dark evil essence disappeared into the walls of the house.

Vince and Anne held their daughter close and both were relieved to have their daughter safe in their arms.

Vince stood up and with Alma in his arms and Anne by his side, they walked out from Alma's room and into their bedroom. As Vince laid Alma on his bed, he heard another scream coming from their son's room. Vince told Anne to stay in their bedroom while he checks on their son Joe. Alma was crying in her mother's arms, and Anne would comfort her child as she await for her husband to return. Vince could hear his son calling out and asking for his father's help. Vince tried to open his son's door, but the door would not open.

"Dad! Hurry please!" cried out Joe.

"I'm coming, son!" shouted his father.

Vince took a step back and then, with all his body weight, he charged toward his son's door. The door swung open and there he saw the dark evil essence coming toward his son. Joe, feeling afraid, wanted to run toward his father but felt incapacitated. His father tried to reach out to his son but the evil essence was preventing Vince from doing so. In the master bedroom where Anne was staying with her daughter, Anne decided to grab the cross from the wall above her dresser and told Alma to go hide inside the closet until she comes back for her. Anne made sure Alma was safe and then walked out from her bedroom, down the hallway, and toward her son's bedroom to help her husband save their son.

There she saw her husband struggling to rescue their son, so Anne took the cross that was blessed in holy water and held it up high toward the evil essence.

"Go back to hell where you came from and leave my family alone!" Anne shouted.

The evil essence disappeared once again into the walls of the home. Vince and Anne then grabbed their children and ran out of the house, they got into their vehicle and drove toward the closest motel. Vince rented a room at the Quality Suites for him and his family for one night.

After paying the clerk behind the desk, Vince picked up his daughter and carried her in his arms while Anne held her son's hand as they walked toward their room. Anne got the children settled and then she sat on the foot of the bed with her husband. Her husband was leaning over, with his head down, his elbows resting on his knees and his hands covering his face. Anne put her arm around her husband and rested her head on his back. They both felt emotionally distressed from the paranormal event that took place that evening.

"We were so lucky to get out of there when we did!" said Vince.

"We are safe and our kids are now safe!" Anne told her husband.

"Tomorrow, we will drive down to St. John Baptist Church and talk to Father Mathews!" Anne suggested.

Vince agreed to what his wife suggested, so they both decided to get what remaining sleep they could before morning.

Chapter 10

In the morning, Anne got the children ready and took them to the car while Vince took the room key and dropped it off to the clerk behind the desk. Before dropping the children off at their grandparents' house, they decided to stop and get breakfast at Sunshine Grill. They sat down in the restaurant for an hour, spending time enjoying their breakfast together. Once they received the bill from their waitress, Vince and Anne dropped their kids off at their grandparent's house.

Vince and Anne then drove to St. John's Baptist Church, to talk to their Minister, Father Mathews. Father Mathews was a Minister who preached every Sunday at St. John Baptist Church. When they arrived at the church, they saw Father Johnson standing by the doorway entrance of the church and handing out flyers to his congregation.

"Father Johnson!" shouted Vince.

"Hello! What can I do for you, Mr. and Mrs. Patterson?" replied Father Johnson.

"Can we speak to you and Father Mathews privately?" asked Vince.

"Of Course! Please, come with me." replied Father Johnson.

As they walked through the front entrance of the church…into the gathering space, the faithful greet one another…they then walked into the Nave where one prays and worships, then walked down the aisle, passed the Alter where the minister does the sermon, and walked into the Clergy room where they found Father Mathews sitting behind his desk, reading the scriptures from his bible. The Clergy room is a room where the priest prepares his scriptures and stores the vestments that he wears during each sermon.

"Hello, Father Mathews!" said Anne.

"Hello!" Father Mathews replied.

"Please, both of you, have a seat." Father Mathews told them.

Vince and Anne sat down in one of the chairs that were in front of Father Mathews's desk.

"What can I do for you Mr. and Mrs. Patterson?" asked Father Mathews.

Vince started explaining to Father Mathews what had been happening in their home and the paranormal events taking place. The priest told them that evil had walked among the earth for centuries and for those that who believed and worship the Lord, our God, will always be protected by him. Father Mathews read some scriptures from the bible and said some prayers with Vince and Anne then, took some holy water and on their foreheads, he placed the sign of the cross using his thumb and blessed Vince and Anne.

"Thank you, Father Mathews!" said Vince.

"Could you Come down and bless our home?" Anne asked Father Mathews.

"Your home needs to be exorcised by a special priest that deals with these situations!" commented Father Mathews.

"I know someone that can help you both!" said Father Mathews.

Father Mathews told the Patterson's that he would call them once he did something, and in the meantime, he told them to stay with one of their family members and not to go back to their home.

Vince and Anne thanked Father Mathews and Father Johnson again and drove back to Vince's parents' house where the children have been staying.

When they arrived, Vinces' mom had dinner ready and was about to place it on the table. While Anne helped her mother-in-law set the table and serve the food, Vince got the kids to wash up and they all sat down at the dinner table. After dinner, Anne helped her mother-in-law clear the table and clean the dishes while Vince and the kids watched television in the family room with their grandfather. It was soon getting late, Anne got the children ready for bed in one of the spare rooms while Vince and his parents stayed up a little longer to watch the 11:00 pm news on television.

After the news, Vince said 'Goodnight!' to his parents and went into the other spare bedroom where Anne was sleeping, and went to sleep for the night.

Chapter 11

A week passed, and Vince and Anne finally received the phone call they'd been waiting for. It was Father Mathews and he told Vince that Father Micheals would be contacting them later in the evening to discuss arrangements. He also mentioned to Vince, the amount of exorcised events that Father Micheals endured and the outcome had always been successful. Vince felt grateful for Father Mathew's help and thanked him before ending the call. Vince explained to Anne what Father Mathews said and both felt positive and felt a sense of reassurance.

The phone rang at 8 o'clock and Vince picked up the phone. It was Father Micheals and he was telling Vince that he and his other colleague will be doing the exercise at their home tomorrow morning and asked Vince to meet them there around 7 o'clock. Vince agreed and thanked Father Micheals before ending the call. Vince told Anne about the conversation he had with Father Micheals and that it would be best for her to stay behind with their kids until he returns.

The next morning, Vince drove down to his house where he met Father Micheals and his colleague Father McCormick.

"Mr. Patterson, I presume?" asked Father Micheals.

"Yes!" replied Vince.

"I like you to meet Father McCormick. He will be assisting me in the exorcism of your home," Father Micheals stated.

Vince greeted the two priests and was then told to stay outside while they cleanse the home.

Father Micheals and Father McCormick gathered the materials they needed from the trunk of their car and entered the house. They started in the basement, both felt the evil around them and the foul decay odor that filled the air, making it hard for them to breathe. Father Micheals opened his bible and read scriptures out loud while Father McCormick took the aspergillum, dipped the end in the base filled with holy water, and sprinkled the consecrated water in the air.

As they spiritually cleanse each room, the lights would flicker, the kitchen cabinet doors would open and slam shut and random objects would fly across the room. When they reached the last room in the basement, a dark ghostly apparition flew past them and went up the stairs to the main level. Father Micheals and Father McCormick, carefully walked up the stairs to the main level of the house.

Father Micheals began reading scriptures from the bible while Father McCormick took the aspergillum once again and sprinkled the consecrated water in the air. The dark evil essence became agitated by the priest and Father Micheals knew that they would have to take cover and shield themselves from what was about to happen next. They both pushed the tall cabinet in the living room from the wall and hid behind it as they continue the exorcism. All the bedroom doors started opening and slamming shut, the dishes in the kitchen cabinet and the utensils from the kitchen drawers flew out across the room and nearly endangering the priest. Finally, Father Micheals was at the end of the scripture in his bible when everything stopped and became very quiet. The priest slowly stood up from behind the tall cabinet and noticed all was calm. As they walked toward the kitchen, standing there in the hallway were the ghostly figures of Clare and Hannah McGreevy.

The two spirits were at peace and were no longer frapped in the evil grips of Charles McGreevy. A light shone down upon Clare and Hannah's apparition as though the gates of heaven had opened up and were welcoming them both. Hannah and Clare's spirits were pulled into the light and both of the priests knew that they were at peace. In the corner of an eye, they both noticed the apparition of Charles McGreevy hovering in the corner of the kitchen, As the evil apparition tried to come toward the priests to harm them, two dark evil shadows came through the floor, as though the gates of hell had opened up. The two dark shadows gabbed Charles McGreevy and pulled him down and into the gates of hell. Once the house was cleansed and all the evil was extinguished, Father Micheals and Father McCormick walked out of the house. They explained the scenario to Vince and got into their car, and drove away.

Vince went into the house and saw that everything they owned was completely destroyed, but he didn't care because it was finally over and the weight he felt was lifted off his shoulders. Vince got into his car and drove back to his parents' house to tell his wife the wonderful news and that they soon can go home.

It took several months of reconstructing and replacing all that was lost but finally, Vince and Anne were able to restore their home. The next few months, the Patterson family placed their home up 'For Sale' and bought another home thirty minutes away. They decided that one paranormal event was enough for them to last a lifetime.